For Rachel Louisa
~ *J.W.*
For the St Agnes fishermen
and young friends
~ *N.R.*

First American edition published in 1998 by
Crocodile Books, USA
An imprint of Interlink Publishing Group, Inc.
99 Seventh Avenue • Brooklyn, New York 11215 and
46 Crosby Street • Northampton, Massachusetts 01060
Text © 1998 Judy Waite
Illustrations © 1998 Neil Reed
Published simultaneously in Great Britain by
Magi Publications, London
ISBN 1-56656-292-9
Printed and bound in Belgium
10 9 8 7 6 5 4 3 2 1

~ The ~
Storm Seal

Judy Waite
illustrated by Neil Reed

Crocodile Books, USA

An imprint of Interlink Publishing Group, Inc.
NEW YORK

The weather was wild. Angry lightning scratched
across the grumbling sky. The waves heaved and
hurled. In the exploding night,
pressed against giant gray rocks,
the seals were huddling.

By morning, the storm had faded.
The wind dropped to a shout, then a whisper.
Along the sand an old man was walking,
clearing trash. And as he searched carefully
among piles of seaweed, something stirred.

Tangled in the knots of an old fishing
line lay a tiny seal pup, barely breathing.
"Poor little thing," said the old man,
wrapping it gently
in his sweater.

A boy playing on the beach spotted the old man.
"It's Peter!" he cried, calling out to his friends.
"I think he's found something."
The retired sailor was well-known in the village
for rescuing hurt animals.

Peter put his fingers to his lips as the children came
near. "Shhh," he whispered gently. "Don't crowd
around. He needs lots of peace and quiet."
The children understood, and watched silently as
Peter carried his precious bundle up the steep path
to his home.

Peter made a place in his kitchen for the baby seal and offered him fish soup from a bottle. But the little pup just closed his eyes and turned away. So Peter sat and stroked his head and sang to him softly all the songs he knew from his days at sea.

By evening, the pup had taken his first spluttering drink. And when the soup was gone, he sucked gently on Peter's hand for comfort, while the velvet night crept softly in through the windows.

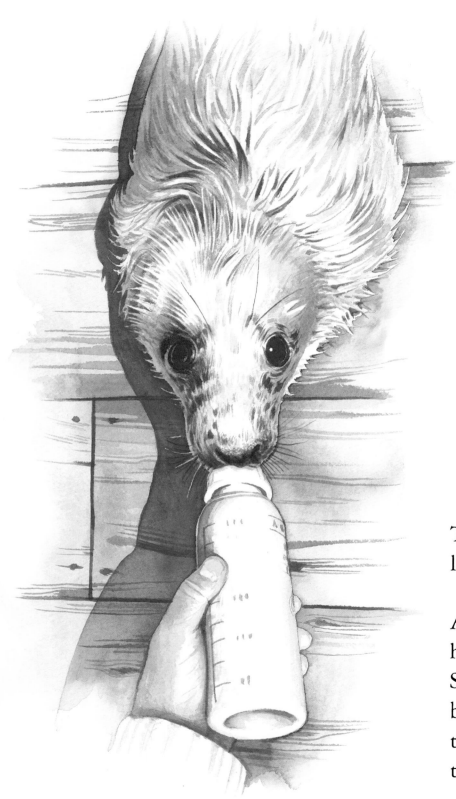

The next morning, the
little seal seemed brighter.

And as the days passed,
he grew stronger still.
Soon, he had lost his white
baby fur and was eating
the fresh fish Peter tossed
to him every morning.

He often followed Peter around, and when the
days grew warmer, he played in the garden with
the other animals.

Now that the seal was better, the children came
to visit him. He rolled on his back and pawed
them with his flipper, like a dog wanting a game.

More and more people came to see the little seal. Peter was glad they were interested. But he was also thankful when the night came and the two of them could enjoy the quiet for a while.

Then, one morning, Peter fell ill.
The doctor came and ordered him to bed.
But Peter was anxious about all his animals.
"Don't worry," the doctor said. "I'll arrange for
someone to help."

And he did. The local people were wonderful.
They shopped and they cleaned, they brushed and
they fed. Every day after school, the children came.
They helped with all the animals, but most of all,
they loved to help with the seal.

One day, the children brought a ball and
taught the seal to balance it on his nose.
They dressed him up in sunglasses, a hat,
and a scarf.

The seal looked funny in his new outfit,
but he didn't look much like a seal any more.

Upstairs, Peter was feeling better. He wondered
what all the noise was about. Slowly, he got up
and went downstairs.

Nobody noticed him as he stood in the doorway.
They were all too busy laughing at the seal.
"Oh no," said Peter, stepping forward. "Remember,
he's a wild animal. He might nip if he gets frightened.
And he's much too special for tricks and toys."
Peter knew now that he had something to get strong for.

Early each morning, Peter rowed out to sea.
He took the seal along, and taught him how to
dive for food among the silver flashes of fish.

One morning, as the soft pink of sunrise still washed
the sky, Peter saw something moving around the rocks.
It was a great colony of seals.
One seal broke away from the others, and swam right
up to the boat. Peter's seal stared hard at the stranger.
"Don't worry," said Peter gently. "It's a friend."

The seal touched Peter
lightly with his nose,
then leaped into the water
with a splash of sparkling
silver. The other seal swam
with him, nudging and
nuzzling him, then dived
suddenly away.

Peter's seal swam
back to the boat.
"It's all right," said
Peter. "It's time for
you to go."
Then Peter's seal
dived after his new
friend, and the game
began.

The two seals raced and chased, they rumbled
and tumbled, deep in the water under the boat.
And Peter rowed back to the shore through
the bright burst of morning.

On the beach, the children were waiting.
They were worried about the seal.
"Look out to sea," said Peter, pointing.
"He's back where he belongs."

The children turned to see two black shapes
bobbing and splashing in the water.
"He has a friend already," said Peter, smiling.
"And see, it looks like they're laughing. It looks
like they're happy."
As they watched the seals slip away into the
distance, Peter and the children were happy, too.